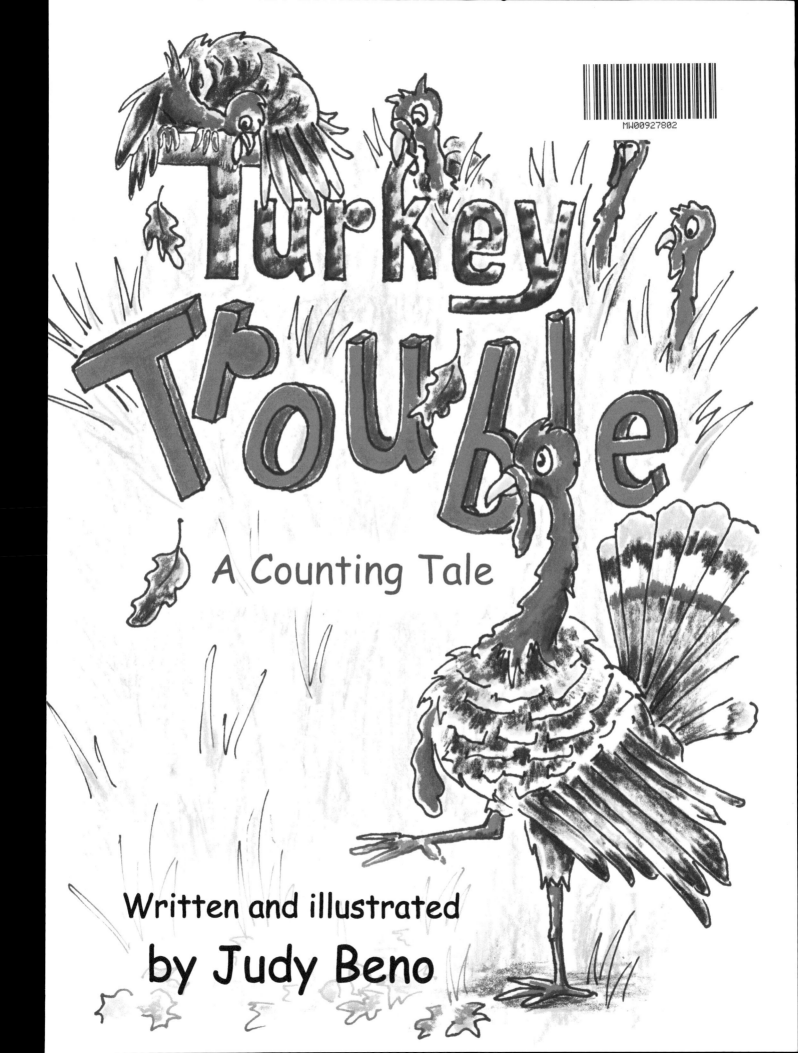

Turkey Trouble

A Counting Tale

Written and illustrated
by Judy Beno

To my grandchildren:
Isaac, Everly and Mae

For other books by
Judy Beno, scan here.

ISBN 978-0-9883914-1-3
Designed by Lisa Blore
Published by ECLECTRY BOOKS

Five plump turkeys,
on a crisp November day,
Strutted through a meadow
till one heard a chipmunk say,

"I think I heard
a hunter
passing by my door."

That turkey

flew into

a

tree,

And

then

there

were . . .

Four feathered turkeys
watched the autumn
leaves fall down,
And nibbled at the
acorns that were strewn
upon the ground.

One heard
a bird,
who passed the word,

"You'll be safer
in a tree!"

He flew up high
as a man passed by

And left

behind the . . .

Three gobbling turkeys,
heads bobbing up and down,
Seemed to hardly notice
that their friends
were not around.

Till one's
sharp eye
caught a
cap go by

And knew
just what
to do.

Behind a bush he slid
and quietly hid,

And
then
there
were
just . . .

Two turkeys wobbled
to the brook to get a drink.
You'd think they'd miss
their other friends,
but turkeys rarely think.

A frightened mouse
went zipping by,

"Hide, turkey,
or you're
done!"

One turkey

flew into

a tree

And

left

behind

just . . .

One turkey
came upon a car,
the likes he'd never known.
He jumped on top.
Perhaps he thought
he'd claim it for
his own.

Then startled by some
footsteps,
That prideful turkey
froze.

The man aimed and

But he caught
the perfect pose.

CPSIA information can be obtained
at www.ICGtesting.com
Printed in the USA
BVHW020218260821
615298BV00001B/1